◁ W9-AKS-745

For Brett, Wolfie, and Wilhelmina,
because I love you
—Aunt Julie

For Alora
—L.P.

Visit us on the Web! randomhousekids.com

Educators and librarians, for a variety of teaching tools, visit us at
RHTeachersLibrarians.com

Library of Congress Cataloging-in-Publication Data
Moore, Julianne.
Freckleface Strawberry and the really big voice /
by Julianne Moore ; illustrated by LeUyen Pham. —
First edition.
pages cm
Summary: After a noisy summer, Freckleface Strawberry and her
friends return to school where the only time they should be loud is
at recess, but Windy Pants Patrick cannot remember to use his indoor
voice, and that comes in handy before the day is through.
ISBN 978-0-385-39203-7 (trade) — ISBN 978-0-375-97370-3 (lib. bdg.) —
ISBN 978-0-385-39204-4 (ebook)
[1. Voice—Fiction. 2. Quietude—Fiction. 3. Schools—Fiction.]
I. Pham, LeUyen, illustrator. II. Title.
PZ7.M78635Ftr 2016 [E]—dc23 2015017130

The illustrations for this book were rendered in
black Japanese brush pen, colored digitally.

Book design by Nicole de las Heras

MANUFACTURED IN CHINA

10 9 8 7 6 5 4 3 2 1

First Edition

JULIANNE MOORE

Freckleface Strawberry
and the
REALLY BIG VOICE

illustrated by
LeUyen Pham

Doubleday Books for Young Readers

Every day in the summer,
Frreckleface Strawberry says,

Noah says,

I CAN
HEAR THE
ICE CREAM
TRUCK!

LET'S RUN THROUGH
THE SPRINKLER!

And Windy Pants Patrick says,

Winnie says,

RACE WITH MEEEEEEEEEEEEEEEEE!!!!!!!

COME AND SEE WHAT I MADE!

And the children sound like . . .

But NOW it is time to go back to school.

And on the playground before class starts,
Freckleface Strawberry says,

I AM A MONSTER!

Noah says,

I AM THE KING
OF FREEZE TAG!

Winnie says,

LET'S MAKE
A PICTURE!

And Windy Pants Patrick says,

WHO WANTS TO PLAY
DODGEBALL?????

And the children on the
playground sound like . . .

. . . until the bell rings and all the children go inside to the classroom.

In the classroom,

Freckleface Strawberry says,

May I please pass out the papers?

Noah says,

I finished my work sheet.

Winnie says,

And the children in the classroom sound like . . .

And Windy Pants Patrick says . . .

And Freckleface Strawberry says,

Shhhhhhhhh, Windy Pants.
You are too loud. Use your
inside voice, please.

And Windy Pants Patrick says,

sorry.

In the lunch room,
Freckleface Strawberry says,

I love lunch.

Noah says,

This is the best part of the day!

Winnie says,

Today I chose pasta!

And all the children in the lunch room sound like . . .

And Windy Pants Patrick says . . .

And the teacher in the lunch room says,

Patrick, keep your voice down.
Please use your inside voice.

And Windy Pants Patrick says,

okay.

In the library, Freckleface Strawberry says,

I want to read about monsters.

Noah says,

I want to read about cars and trucks.

Winnie says,

I want to read about art.

And everybody says,

WINDY PANTS PATRICK!!!!!!
PLEASE BE QUIET. This is a library!
Inside voice, please!

And Windy Pants just nods his head.

In music class,
Freckleface Strawberry says,

La la la

Noah says,

Loo loo loo

Winnie says,

Lee lee lee

And the teacher says,

nothing.

And Freckleface Strawberry, Noah,
and Winnie look at Windy Pants Patrick.

And Windy Pants Patrick
raises his hand and says . . .

I have a big voice.

La

LOO

LEEEEE

And the children sound like music.